True Scary Short Stories To Read Vol. IV

by

M. A Munslow

M. A Munslow

Copyright © 2022 M. A. Munslow
All rights reserved

The characters and events portrayed in this book are fictitious. Any similarity to real persons, living or dead, is coincidental and not intended by the author.

No part of this book may be reproduced, or stored in a retrieval system, or transmitted in any form or by any means, electronic, mechanical, photocopying, recording, or otherwise, without express written permission of the publisher.

True Scary Short Stories to Read Vol. IV

Contents

Story 1 _____ *4*

Story 2 _____ *6*

Story 3 _____ *9*

Story 4 _____ *12*

Story 5 _____ *15*

Story 6 _____ *26*

Story 7 _____ *28*

Story 8 _____ *32*

Story 9 _____ *34*

Story 10 _____ *36*

M. A Munslow

Story 1

One day, my friend Austin asked me, "Brandon, what do you think is the most beautiful thing in the world?" I pondered for a moment and replied, "Well, flowers, nature, or women." Austin then said expressionlessly, "The most beautiful thing in the world is the sight of someone dying, their desperate plea for help. No one else in this world possesses a more desperate heart than at that moment. Isn't it truly beautiful? And when they face their impending death, they fight for their lives with everything they have. It's the moment they act most passionately in their lives. If they don't face death, they will live their lives without experiencing such passion. It's truly tragic. That's why every human being must be murdered."

I was taken aback by his passionate and chilling gaze. Yes, he was sincere. In an attempt to change the somber atmosphere, I forced a smile and said, "That's an interesting thought. So, does that mean you have to be murdered too?" He glared at me and replied, "No, I have to stay alive until the end. I have to kill them all." And then he said something else, "Brandon, let's save humanity together. Put an end to their lifeless existence and create a climax in their lives, just like a flower that blooms and then withers. And the only way to do that is through murder."

Fear gripped me. I wanted to refuse, but when I saw the madness in his eyes, I couldn't bring myself to do it. If I refused, he would surely kill me. A few days later, he showed me a video and said, "Brandon, take look. Another masterpiece has been born." In the video, a person was hanging upside down. Below them was a large drum filled with water, labeled as hydrochloric acid. The person was screaming for help. Austin said, "Look into this person's eyes. Have you ever seen such a desperate gaze? People in today's world have empty eyes, as if everything bores them. But in reality, they all had eyes as vivid as this person. Isn't it truly beautiful?" He shouted with exhilaration in his voice, as if roaring in triumph.

I trembled in fear as he delightedly replayed the video over and over again. Eventually, the person was dissolved in the acid, and Austin cheered and applauded. "Ah, it's truly perfect."

In the end, I went home and reported it to the police, and he was arrested. He sent me a letter from prison, saying, "Brandon, because of you, my plan to save the world has been ruined. Just watch, this world will turn into hell. You will feel the weight of your mistake deeply. Or, you can come to your senses now and execute my plan instead. Then this world can be saved. Kill all those with lifeless eyes and bring vitality back to this world."

M. A Munslow

Story 2

One day, my friend Ricky asked me to accompany him to a secret underground zoo that very few people knew about. He claimed it was a unique place where human and animal genes were combined to create extraordinary creatures. Intrigued and excited, I agreed to join him on this mysterious adventure.

Upon arriving at the entrance, we were greeted by a bustling crowd and guided by the staff. They welcomed us to the "Human Zoo" and emphasized the importance of signing a confidential oath, promising never to reveal what we would witness. It was explained that anyone who broke this oath would become prey to the beasts within.

Descending ten floors underground in an elevator, we arrived at a massive glass wall that showcased living creatures beyond our imagination. The first creature I saw was a towering figure covered in crocodile skin, standing on short limbs and glaring at us with yellow reptilian eyes. We encountered more astonishing beings, including an eagle-like creature with a human-like face and immense wingspan.

As we continued our journey, the zookeepers fed the creatures, which captivated everyone's attention. The spectacle was both unbelievable and shocking as we encountered hybrid creatures with features ranging from black panther heads to snake heads and tiger-human hybrids. They eagerly pounced on the glass, eliciting gasps from the onlookers.

True Scary Short Stories to Read Vol. IV

Amidst the wonder, someone tried to capture the spectacle with a hidden camera. However, a vigilant security guard swiftly confiscated the camera, ensuring the secrecy of the zoo remained intact. The staff then announced the arrival of the main event, heightening the anticipation of the crowd.

To our horror, the zookeepers appeared dragging a person in a cage filled with tiger-men. The helpless individual was thrown into the cage, and within seconds, a tiger-man tore them apart. The shocking revelation followed that the victim was not a real human, but a clone created through genetic recombination. The senseless brutality left me in disbelief, but others seemed unfazed, even expressing interest in owning such creatures as pets.

Aghast by the immoral activities, I decided to take action and reported the zoo to the authorities. However, to my dismay, I found myself abducted by zoo employees disguised as police officers. They took me to a laboratory within the zoo, where the doctor behind these heinous experiments confronted me, threatening to alter my genetic structure and transform me into a beast.

Days passed in captivity, enduring the doctor's relentless study of my DNA alongside that of various animals. Eventually, government agents stormed the zoo, arresting all the staff and doctors, freeing me from their clutches. I returned home, eager to share my harrowing experience with my family, but their disbelief overshadowed my story. Strangely, the media remained silent about the incident, and men in black suits warned me to keep the events secret.

The zoo vanished mysteriously, leaving no trace of its existence. The fate of the unique creatures and what truly transpired within those walls remains unknown, hidden from the world's knowledge.

True Scary Short Stories to Read Vol. IV

Story 3

This is a creepy story of what I experienced while camping with a friend of mine five years ago. We ventured into a deep, unknown valley, driving for over 10 hours and hiking for another five hours to reach our destination. As we arrived, a majestic landscape of nature unfolded before us, with clear water, mountains, and fresh air. It felt like we had stumbled upon a paradise fit for gods.

My friend, Brad, and I began fishing, enjoying the tranquility of the surroundings. However, after a while, I heard a strange sound. At first, I thought it was just a bug or a bird, but as it continued, it sounded more like a person's voice. I turned to Brad and asked if he thought someone else had come to this secluded place. Brad assured me that he was the only one who knew about this spot.

Curiosity turned into alarm when I noticed a man in the grass, staring at us. He wore tattered clothing that appeared to be made of leather. His blank stare and the odd noises he made, reminiscent of insects, sent shivers down our spines. In his hand, he held what looked like raw meat from some unknown animal. Startled, I shouted and demanded to know who he was, but he remained silent, disappearing into the forest.

Anxious and unsettled, we contemplated whether we should abandon our camping trip. However, the long journey prevented us from returning home, so we decided to stay. Gradually, we became immersed in the real and enjoyable aspects of camping, eventually falling asleep.

M. A Munslow

In the middle of the night, I was abruptly awakened by high-pitched screaming. I realized it was Brad howling in agony. Hastily, I rushed to his tent, only to witness the horrifying sight of the man I had seen earlier, accompanied by several others, gripping Brad's limbs and pulling with an unnatural frenzy. Their attempts to tear his limbs apart were met with bone-chilling sounds of bones and cartilage being torn.

Fear consumed me as I fumbled to dial 9-1-1 on my cell phone, but my voice failed me. Gasping for breath, I barely managed to speak, knowing that help would arrive too late. In a desperate attempt to save myself, I fled into the woods, leaving behind the tragic fate of Brad. Tears streamed down my face as I ran frantically, my bare feet suffering from cuts and bloodshed.

Eventually, the sirens of the police were heard, and they arrived at the scene. Shocked by the gruesome sight of Brad's torn limbs, they immediately began their investigation. A few days later, I learned from the police that the culprits had been apprehended. They were a family living deep in the mountains, disconnected from civilization, surviving by grazing on grass and hunting animals.

This family's isolation had given them an extraordinary grip strength, allowing them to rip Brad's limbs apart with their bare hands. Their ability to communicate had significantly degraded, making it difficult for the authorities to gather information. When questioned about the whereabouts of Brad's limbs, they gestured towards their own stomachs indicating that they had consumed them. In a chilling display, they even pointed at the officers' limbs, indicating a desire to feast on them.

The family members were eventually incarcerated, but due to their potential danger to other prisoners, they were kept in complete isolation. The horror of that fateful night still haunts me, a chilling reminder of the depths of darkness that can lurk in the most unexpected places.

M. A Munslow

Story 4

I live in an apartment, and one day I started hearing a man swearing every morning at 4 am from the upstairs unit. I endured it once or twice, but it became increasingly annoying to hear it at the same time every day. Finally, I mustered the courage to go upstairs. On the front door of the unit, there was a sign that read "Exorcist." I knocked on the door, and after a while, a man emerged. However, the moment he saw me, his expression turned sour, and he asked, "What is a sane man, not possessed by a ghost, doing here?"

I couldn't help but notice that his pupils were abnormally small, his eyes mostly white, and a cold air seemed to emanate from his house like a refrigerator. Startled, I tried to maintain my composure and explained, "I live downstairs. Why do you always lose your temper at four in the morning? It's so noisy that I can't sleep." He responded, "Four in the morning is when evil spirits run rampant the most. So, I exterminate them at that time. I have no choice. The spirits I exercise are infesting this house. Get out quickly before they attach themselves to you."

I glanced around his house, but it was eerily quiet inside. However, before he closed the door, I distinctly heard multiple voices conversing, which struck me as odd. He pushed me away and slammed the door shut. Feeling unsettled and with goosebumps on my skin, I returned to my own apartment.

True Scary Short Stories to Read Vol. IV

From that day on, I started hearing a soft singing sound throughout the day. It started faint but grew louder, seemingly closer to my ears. I felt like I was losing my mind. Reluctantly, I went back to the Exorcist, who, upon seeing me, clicked his tongue and said, "As expected, you're possessed by a ghost. The ghost is singing a song of death in your ears." However, I couldn't fully believe him, so I returned home.

But then, even more unsettling things started happening. I woke up in the middle of the night choking, with no one around, and a persistent stuffiness in my nose that wouldn't clear up. Another time, while driving, a mysterious hand pressed down on my foot, causing the car to accelerate uncontrollably. Only by summoning all my strength did I manage to release my foot and survive.

One dawn, as I went to get water, something flashed on the floor. When I turned on the light, I discovered a kitchen knife beneath my feet. Since I live alone, nobody would have left a knife there. I started fearing that something serious would happen if these occurrences continued. Thus, I decided to visit the Exorcist once again.

I knocked on his door, and he looked at me, remarking, "You're not dead yet, to survive." Finally, I mustered the courage to ask him for an exorcism. We went to his house at 4 am, and the Exorcist began reciting prayers, whispering them rapidly into my ear. He said, "Come with me to the afterlife. Let's live happily together forever in the world of the dead. Come with me."

M. A Munslow

What sent shivers down my spine was that upon hearing his voice, I felt a strange sense of contentment and found myself replying, "Okay, let's go together." In response, the Exorcist yelled at me with a thunderous voice, and gradually, the voice in my ear faded away. The exorcism continued throughout the night, and by the break of dawn, the Exorcist declared that he had successfully expelled all the evil spirits. He warned me never to return.

I returned home, and though I still heard the man swearing upstairs every morning, I dared not go there. Fortunately, nothing else happened after that. However, from time to time, I hear knocking on my front door, even though no one is standing outside—a haunting reminder of the foreign and inexplicable events I experienced.

Story 5

A few days ago, in my remote forest house, I started hearing a faint scratching noise coming from the walls. I searched the entire house, thinking it might be a wild animal, but there was no trace of any creature, and the sound only grew louder with each passing day. After four days of searching, I finally pinpointed the source of the sound.

While I was busy with carpentry in the yard, my saw suddenly broke. I headed to the basement, a place I hadn't been in a long time, to retrieve a spare saw. As I rummaged through my dusty toolbox, shining my flashlight, I heard the very sound that had been haunting me for days—coming from right behind me. I was taken aback, my whole body stiffening as I quickly turned around to shine the flashlight in the direction of the sound. However, to my surprise, there was nothing there.

I approached the wall and pressed my ear against it. Astonishingly, the sound was coming from the wall itself, at a very close distance. It resembled the noise of something scratching the wall with a sharp tool, but it didn't sound like a wild animal. The scratching came in regular intervals, making the situation all the more eerie and terrifying. Unsure of what lay behind the concrete wall, I felt a deep sense of unease and fear. I decided I couldn't stay in that house any longer.

In a hurry, I packed my belongings and left, immediately calling the police to report the scratching noise within the basement walls. Their response was dismissive, suggesting it was probably just a wild animal, and they couldn't prioritize responding to mere noise complaints. Left with no choice, I left the forest and spent the night at the nearest motel.

Reluctantly, I returned home the next day, filled with trepidation. However, upon my arrival, I discovered a scene of chaos. It looked as if someone had broken into my kitchen and living room, leaving mud everywhere. The refrigerator stood wide open, its contents missing, and the floor was covered in countless footprints that led straight to the basement. Gripping my gun tightly, I cautiously descended into the basement, only to be met with an astonishing sight.

There was a massive hole in the basement wall, its depth impossible to discern in the dim light. Alarmed, I immediately called the police, and after a while, they arrived, initiating a thorough search of the house. Numerous fingerprints were found, but what startled the investigators was that none of the fingerprints matched any known records. Despite their efforts, they couldn't identify any of the intruders. One police officer noted that they estimated a total of eight intruders, but even if they traced all the fingerprints, none could be matched or identified. Additionally, the shape of the fingerprints was highly unique.

The officer peered into the hole in the basement wall, using a flashlight. After a moment, he spoke, "The depth of this hole is immeasurable, and it's too dangerous for anyone to venture inside for an investigation. We've never encountered a situation like this before. It will take some time to organize a proper search party. How about you move out for now?"

True Scary Short Stories to Read Vol. IV

Having spent my entire life as a carpenter, cutting trees in the forest, I had nowhere else to go. Fearful but with no alternative, I decided to seal the hole and continue living in the house. Once the police had departed, I found myself alone in the house. I covered the hole with a sturdy wooden board, firmly nailing it down, and locked the basement door. Who were those eight people who broke into my house? The house resumed its silent demeanor, and the scratching noise from the walls ceased for several days.

As time passed, the memory of the incident faded, and I gradually grew less anxious. However, a month later, upon returning home from the woods where I had been cutting trees, I heard an unfamiliar noise coming from the basement. It was unlike anything I had ever heard before—an eerie, snake-like sound. Holding my gun tightly, I cautiously opened the basement door. Suddenly, something lunged at me, grasping onto my body and strangling me. It was a grotesque creature with a bald head, its skin translucent, revealing intricate blood vessels. Its appearance bore a resemblance to that of a human, but with no trace of black in its eyes. Before I knew it, several other creatures surrounded me.

When I regained consciousness, I realized some time had passed. I felt the excruciating pain from my chafed back, and as I looked around, I saw the creatures grabbing my legs, dragging me into the subterranean depths. They emitted eerie hissing sounds, their translucent bodies emitting an eerie green glow in the darkness. The narrow underground passage gradually expanded, allowing an adult to stand and walk.

M. A Munslow

Countless creatures had gathered, crawling toward me, their touch unsettling as they began to caress me.

The creatures lifted me up and led me deeper into the tunnel, where I saw one creature sitting with its head hanging low. It was the leader among them, with a wrinkled, hunched body. Slowly, it lifted its head, fixing its eyes upon me. Its eyes resembled those of a human, albeit with blurry black irises. The creature's eyes widened as it saw me, and it started making strange noises, speaking in a language I couldn't comprehend.

Perplexed, I asked, "What did you say?" The creature continued muttering incomprehensible words, while the others watched us, holding their breath. I wondered if this language truly existed, so I pulled out my phone from my pocket, intending to use a voice translation app. To my dismay, the translator failed to recognize the creature's words. Determined to document their speech, I switched to the voice recorder and captured the creature's utterances.

Finally, the creature, which had been muttering in an unknown language, emitted a hiss, prompting the other creatures to rush toward me, offering various insects, dead moles, and tree roots. It seemed as though they were sharing their food with me. At that moment, I realized that they had no intention of harming me. I signaled that I wouldn't partake in their offering, and they hesitantly backed away. Soon after, they brought forth a female creature, attempting to thrust her upon me. With a mix of astonishment and fear, I managed to shake her off. Overwhelmed by the frightful situation, I cried out, begging them to allow me to return home

True Scary Short Stories to Read Vol. IV

The creatures then guided me back through the tunnel we had traversed. Walking through the long and winding passage, relying on the green glow emitted by the creatures, proved arduous in the pitch darkness. After numerous twists and turns, I finally emerged from the hole in the basement of my house. The female creature crawled out as well and began hissing and scurrying around the basement.

I swiftly escaped the basement, locking the door behind me. I immediately called the police to explain the situation. Soon, they arrived along with a search party. Carefully, they opened the basement door, and at that moment, the female creature lunged at me, gripping onto me tightly. I screamed in terror, and the police forcibly removed the creature from my body, striking its head with a club. As they dragged the lifeless creature outside, white smoke suddenly billowed from its transparent skin. Exposed to sunlight, it rapidly blackened and perished in agonizing pain.

From that day forward, I underwent a lengthy investigation about what I had witnessed underground. Many individuals involved frequented my house, and a police line surrounded the property. The corpse of the deceased creature underwent an autopsy, revealing organs resembling those of a human within its translucent skin, although lacking lungs. Gill-like openings were pierced diagonally along its ribs, leading experts to speculate that they had adapted to the underground environment, breathing through these gills. The creatures' eyesight had deteriorated, explaining their lack of irises and their struggle to perceive objects in the presence of light.

M. A Munslow

I submitted the file containing the recorded voice of the creature on my cell phone to the police, and numerous historians gathered to analyze the language. Astonishingly, it turned out to be an ancient North American Native American language, unspoken by modern society. Translated, the message conveyed, "You are our first ancestor. We hid underground to outlive the war, surviving generation after generation for a very long time. If I die, there will be no one to pass down our language. Teach our language to these people."

The creatures, it seemed, were natives who had taken refuge underground thousands of years ago to escape an unknown war. Over the course of time, their bodies had evolved to adapt to the subterranean environment, transforming them into the peculiar beings I encountered. The government strictly controlled knowledge of their existence, as it could have significant social implications. I, too, was required to sign a memorandum, pledging not to disclose all the details.

My wounds from the creature's bite were stitched up at the hospital and treated regularly, gradually healing. The nightmarish memories of that day began to fade. Looking at myself in the mirror, I sighed in relief, observing no visible traces of the creature's attack. Stripping off my clothes to take a shower, I made a shocking discovery—strange holes pierced my ribs. I examined myself in astonishment, realizing that some parts of my body had turned transparent, revealing intricate blue blood vessels.

True Scary Short Stories to Read Vol. IV

Rushed back to the hospital, my body attracted the attention of all the doctors. They were shocked, stating that the disease I had was unprecedented and unlike anything they had encountered before. It was at that moment I understood that my body was gradually transforming into a creature after being bitten. Upon returning home, I endured the agony of witnessing the terrible changes occurring in my appearance.

After much contemplation, I mustered the courage to confront my reflection in the mirror. The black irises of my eyes had faded, and my skin had turned transparent, causing unbearable prickling and pain when exposed to ultraviolet rays. I realized that I could no longer continue my life as a carpenter, cutting trees or venturing beyond my yard. Driven by intuition, I recognized that the only way for me to survive was to venture into the hole in the basement.

Breaking through the sealed basement door, I commenced drilling through the concrete that had been used to fill the hole. I persevered, drilling continuously for a week, until I finally heard sounds from outside the basement. Squeezing my body through the hole, I disregarded the shouting of the police officers, eager to reach the world beyond.
As I emerged from the hole, I could hear the frantic voices of the police officers trying to dissuade me. But I was resolute in my decision to explore further, driven by a mix of curiosity and desperation. My body, now exhibiting the telltale signs of transformation, moved with an otherworldly agility as I navigated through the darkness.

The subterranean world I entered was unlike anything I had ever seen. Bioluminescent fungi adorned the walls, casting an ethereal glow that illuminated my path. The air felt thick with mystery and an ancient energy that seemed to resonate with every step I took.

Guided by an unexplainable intuition, I followed the faint sound of echoing whispers. The voices grew louder as I delved deeper into the labyrinthine tunnels. It was a chorus of forgotten souls, their words merging into an incomprehensible symphony. With each passing moment, the weight of their existence pressed upon me, filling me with a sense of responsibility to uncover their story.

Eventually, I arrived at a vast chamber, adorned with intricate carvings and symbols that pulsated with a faint, iridescent glow. At its center stood an ancient altar, adorned with offerings and relics of a forgotten era. The whispers intensified, urging me forward.

As I approached the altar, the murmurs transformed into discernible words in my mind. They spoke of a long-lost civilization that had sought refuge in the depths of the earth to escape the horrors of war. These creatures were the remnants of a once-proud people, clinging to their identity and struggling to survive in a world long forgotten.

Their request was simple yet profound. They sought a way to share their language and their story with the surface dwellers, to bridge the gap between their hidden realm and the world above. It was an opportunity to honor their existence and ensure their legacy endured.

Moved by their plight, I pledged to fulfill their request. But I knew it would not be easy. Society above ground was not prepared for the existence of these extraordinary beings. Fear and ignorance would likely overshadow understanding and acceptance.

Returning to the surface, I found myself torn between the two worlds. The weight of their presence and the responsibility they had entrusted upon me weighed heavily on my shoulders. It was a delicate balance between preserving their secrets and advocating for their recognition.

Through tireless efforts, I sought out scholars, linguists, and historians who could help me decipher the language and understand the cultural significance of the creatures below. I reached out to open-minded individuals who shared a fascination with the unknown, hoping to find allies in this unique endeavor.

Together, we worked relentlessly, conducting research, documenting every detail, and attempting to bridge the gap between these two distinct worlds. It was an arduous task, as skepticism and disbelief often met our efforts. But we persevered, knowing that the creatures' story deserved to be told.

As word spread, a small but dedicated community of supporters emerged. They shared our passion for exploration and understanding, driven by a desire to embrace the wonders of the hidden realm beneath our feet. Through lectures, exhibitions, and immersive experiences, we endeavored to shed light on the existence of these remarkable beings.

M. A Munslow

Gradually, society began to shift its perception. Fear turned into curiosity, ignorance transformed into enlightenment. The creatures, once confined to the shadows, were now recognized as a vital part of our shared history. They became ambassadors of a forgotten era, fostering a newfound connection between our worlds.

Years passed, and the creatures that had once inhabited the depths became celebrated figures in cultural exchanges and academic discussions. Their language, once on the brink of extinction, flourished once more as scholars delved deep into its complexities and nuances.

In time, I came to understand that my transformation was not a curse but a remarkable gift—a bridge between two realms, a living testament to the resilience and adaptability of the creatures that dwelled below. I became a symbol of their existence, a living embodiment of their legacy.

Today, as I stand on the precipice of both worlds, I can't help but feel a sense of awe and gratitude. The journey has been long and arduous, but the reward has been immeasurable. The creatures that once haunted my nightmares are now my comrades, partners in unraveling the mysteries that lie beneath the surface.

The tale of my encounter with the underground realm and the beings that reside there continues to captivate the imagination of people worldwide. It serves as a reminder that there are still unexplored realms waiting to be discovered and embraced. And as I embark on my next adventure, armed with newfound knowledge and understanding, I do so with an open heart and a deep reverence for the hidden wonders that lie beneath our feet.

M. A Munslow

Story 6

In 2015, a chilling winter night, I, a young mother with two girls under the age of 10, was busy preparing dinner at home. My kids were playing upstairs, and my husband had left for work early in the morning and wouldn't be back until midnight. It seemed like a typical day.

Around 7 pm, as I was engrossed in cooking, the doorbell suddenly rang. I found myself alone on the first floor of our house. The kitchen was across the hallway from the front door, and as I turned to see who was there, my eyes fell upon the figure of a thin, frail man wearing loose clothes. Despite the possibility of him being a neighbor or delivery person, the shape of his figure was unfamiliar and sent shivers down my spine. I wasn't expecting any packages either. The question of who could possibly be at my house during that time haunted me.

With cautious steps, I approached the door, hoping to catch a glimpse of the person outside through the window. However, the window on our door had a thick, patterned glass, rendering it impossible to identify the visitor. I retraced my steps to the light switch a few feet away and turned on the hallway light, followed by the porch light. In an instant, the man dropped to the floor, and I found myself frozen in fear. The illumination allowed for clearer visibility, and I could see the man hiding beneath the bench on our porch. What was his intention? What should I do?

I pondered my next move when I noticed that there was not only a man hiding at our door but also a getaway car parked in our driveway. Our neighborhood fostered close-knit relationships, and we all knew each other well. Instinctively, I dialed my neighbor's number, who resided across the street, and urgently asked him to check if anything seemed amiss outside my door. Unfortunately, he couldn't gather any useful information. Faced with uncertainty, I decided to take matters into my own hands and called the local police station, requesting them to drive by and investigate the situation.

For what felt like an eternity, I anxiously stood in the hallway, waiting for any sign of movement. Finally, I heard a commotion at the front door. The car parked in my driveway sped away and arrived at another house on my street. Simultaneously, the man dashed towards the same house. Bewildered by the turn of events, I couldn't fathom the exact circumstances. Shortly after, I saw a police car pass by, and everything seemed normal again. Later, I discovered that the house the man had fled to was notorious for drug-related activities. I can only assume that the man had mistakenly targeted our house, but the harrowing experience continues to haunt me. What compelled him to hide at my door in the first place? To this day, I wonder about the potential outcome if I had opened that door.

M. A Munslow

Story 7

I was younger, around 18 years old, back in 2015. Even now, at 37, I'm still freaked out by what happened and have recurring nightmares about it. It feels like my life is forever changed, but no one believes me. This is why you should never trust what you see.

I took up a pet sitting job for an elderly couple over the summer. They appeared to be around 80 years old, so I didn't think there was anything sketchy or dangerous about it. It was a simple task of watching their cat while they went on a three-day vacation. They only instructed me to feed the cat every seven to nine hours. It seemed like easy money.

On the day I went to their house, I gathered my belongings from the car, including flashlights to navigate their dimly lit house and some extra clothes. As I stepped inside, a musty smell greeted me. It was the first odd occurrence. Despite the house appearing clean and tidy, the scent lingered faintly. I brushed it off and continued.

The elderly couple showed me around their decently sized house with four bedrooms and three bathrooms. The floors were carpeted, and the decorations had a modern touch, surprising for their age. The old woman took me aside to show me where I would be sleeping. The room was nice, but the musty smell was slightly worse there, and the carpet seemed lighter than the rest of the house. I dismissed these details foolishly ignoring my instincts.

They also informed me that their son lived in the house, his room located in the basement. They warned me that he never left his room and that it was off-limits due to his sensitivity. Thirty minutes after they left, I found myself alone with their son. Initially, everything went smoothly for about two hours until something peculiar occurred.

Sitting on the bottom floor, watching TV, I heard a loud slam coming from the basement. Normally, this would have scared me, but I knew their son was down there, so I brushed it off, although it was unsettling. Shortly after, I heard the basement door forcefully swing open. This confused me because if he indeed lived there, why would he slam the door? I let it go, assuming he had come upstairs to get a snack. I decided to check on him, despite the old woman's warning.

I got up, trying not to make any noise, and approached the basement door. To my surprise, the door was wide open, and the stairs leading down were enveloped in complete darkness. No windows, no light anywhere. At that moment, I assumed he had come up from the basement. Thinking he might be in the kitchen, I proceeded towards it. It's important to note that I didn't hear him enter the kitchen; I just assumed he did.

As I turned the corner into the kitchen, there he stood. He had dark brown hair, brown eyes, and appeared to be African-American in his early twenties. He was quite handsome, which somewhat diminished my sense of caution. I took a tentative step forward, and he turned his head towards me. Nothing seemed particularly strange except for the fact that he didn't speak or make any noise. However, what caught my attention were the objects in his hands—a long rope and a kitchen knife. After glancing at me, he whispered, "Basement."

Curiosity clouded my judgment, as this was a small town in 1990, where there weren't many defining factors to identify bad people like stalkers or killers. Besides, the elderly couple didn't strike me as the type to harbor a wanted criminal. I walked away, disregarding the warning. Unlike the saying, "Curiosity killed the cat," in this case, curiosity saved me momentarily.

While passing by the basement, his words echoed in my mind, igniting a growing sense of unease. Something was off, and it all seemed connected to that basement. Retrieving the flashlight I had brought with me, I descended the stairs. The basement wasn't large, containing only a couch in one corner, a coffee table, and an adjacent bedroom. However, the overwhelming stench permeated the air—a mix of rotten eggs and the muskiness that pervaded the entire house. Despite the repugnant odor, my curiosity pushed me forward.

I opened the bedroom door and was confronted with a horrifying sight. A man lay on the floor, surrounded by a pool of blood. He was tightly bound with rope, and a kitchen knife was embedded in the wall nearby. The scene made my eyes well up with tears due to the overpowering stench. Bugs and maggots crawled everywhere. But what truly chilled me to the bone was the realization that the person I saw in the kitchen was the same person lying on the ground—a mirror image. Same shirt, same pants, the same everything. I stood there, horrified and dazed until a maggot landed on me, jolting me back to reality. Without hesitation, I sprinted out of the house, never running faster in my life.

Living too far away, I knocked on the nearest house, seeking refuge from exhaustion. I relayed the horrifying events to the occupants before passing out. They later informed me that the elderly couple had murdered three people in the bedroom where I had been sleeping. That explained why the carpet appeared lighter—they had bleached the entire room. The musty smell wasn't as potent because they had killed their victims hours before my arrival and stuffed their bodies in the closet. The first victim was their son, whom they had bound and killed five days prior. I can't fully comprehend what transpired in that house, but I hope the elderly couple received the punishment they deserved.

M. A Munslow

Story 8

I work as a businessman in Morocco and was sent on a business trip to Nigeria on January 26, 2022. Although I wasn't thrilled about traveling again, I had no choice. I packed my bags and headed to the airport. Upon landing in Nigeria, I was escorted to a luxurious hotel room where they assured me of its safety. However, I was disinterested in their assurances. All I wanted was to finish the business deal and leave.

The next day, I woke up and went to the company to attend the meeting and sign the contract. The day seemed to drag on, but I was relieved when it finally ended. Returning to my ground floor room, I swiped my card, entered, and locked the door behind me. After freshening up and packing my belongings for departure the next day, I went to bed at 11 pm.

At 3 am on January 28, I woke up and decided to use the restroom. When I finished, I went to the dispenser to get some water. As I was about to take a sip, I glanced at the window and noticed the curtains slightly pushed aside. To my surprise, I saw a girl, around six years old, in a gown standing near a tree not far from my window. She just stood there, staring at me. I sighed and checked the time, which read 3:10 am. Concerned, I called out to her, "Hey, kid! It's dangerous to be out there alone. Return to your room." I turned away, assuming she would go back, but something felt off. I glanced at the window again and this time it wasn't the girl but a little boy staring back at me. I cursed in frustration and shouted, gripping the window pane, "It's too late for pranks! Kids, get back to your rooms!" In anger, I turned to leave, but then I remembered that I had left the window open. When I turned to close it, my eyes widened, and I gasped in horror. The hairs on my skin stood on end. This time, it wasn't a child but a dog standing in the same spot, staring directly into my room. Fear overwhelmed me. I slammed the window shut, locked it, and ran back to my bed. Trembling, I covered myself with the blanket, trying to calm my racing heart. Eventually, fear overtook me, and I passed out.

I woke up at 8 am the next morning, dressed quickly, and prepared for my flight, which was scheduled for 10:30 am. As I walked toward the door, I noticed something that triggered my memory. It all turned out to be a dream, but one thing troubled me—I found the door unlocked and slightly open. My heart raced in fear. I checked all my belongings and realized that nothing was missing. I distinctly remember locking the door before going to bed. What happened? The hotel security reviewed the CCTV cameras but found nothing. At that point, I had no interest in staying any longer. I thanked the receptionist, left the hotel, and boarded my flight back to Morocco safely.

Not a day goes by that I don't think about what happened in Nigeria. What exactly transpired at that supposedly luxurious hotel.

M. A Munslow

Story 9

My name is Juliana. I am currently 13 years old, with dark brown hair and dark brown eyes. I will admit that this isn't the scariest of stories, but it still confuses me to this day. This incident took place in mid-2017. For some context, my mom has a job that requires her to travel frequently. A few days before this happened, she informed me that she had a trip and would be gone for a few days. I was pretty sad, but I knew it was just a business trip and she would be back soon.

A few days passed, and my sister's dad and I were having fun going out, watching movies, and enjoying snacks – our usual routine. Finally, the day arrived when my mom would be back. However, I had been having trouble sleeping for a few weeks, so I was lying in bed, unable to sleep. That's when I heard the door open and footsteps. But here's where things got weird – the footsteps sounded like a man's, and then they abruptly stopped. I was very confused but dismissed it as noise from our neighbors. We lived in a townhouse, so it made sense in my nine-year-old mind.

Around 2 am, I heard footsteps again, but this time they were a woman's. I saw a woman at the top of the stairs, wearing a pencil skirt that looked identical to my mom's favorite type of skirt. Naturally, I thought it was my mom returning. I wanted to go up and hug her, but I had a feeling she was exhausted, so I let her walk into the bedroom. However, about an hour later, I heard the door downstairs open. I went downstairs and turned on the light, only to find my mom standing there. She asked me why I was still awake, and I lied, saying I was waiting for her.

I still think about this incident from time to time. Inside, I was panicking. Who or what was that lady, and why did she look like my mom? Did I miss her so much that I started hallucinating? I am so grateful that I decided to stay in my bed and not go up to the lady. I still wonder what I would have seen if I had gone up to her.

M. A Munslow

Story 10

My name is Kushi, and I'm a 17-year-old living in Delhi, India. This incident took place a few months ago. On a crowded evening, after returning from my coaching classes, I decided to book a cab instead of taking the bus due to exhaustion. The distance between my home and the classes was around 21 miles, which usually took about one and a half to two hours to cover.

While in the cab, suddenly, it started shaking and eventually stopped just a mile away from my destination. Since it was dark, the surroundings seemed unfamiliar and the journey appeared longer than usual. Considering the late hour, I made the decision to walk home. As I began walking, I noticed a girl of similar age sitting behind some bushes nearby.

Curiosity got the better of me, and I approached the girl to offer assistance. She lifted her head and in a soft voice, expressed gratitude for my concern. She explained that she had injured her leg while walking and requested my handkerchief to clean the wound. Wanting to help, I asked if she had informed her family about the situation. She assured me that she had already contacted them, and they would be arriving soon. However, the pain was unbearable, and she needed to cover the wound urgently.

I rummaged through my bag, intending to provide her with my handkerchief. Just as I was about to hand it to her, an elderly man appeared, grabbing my arm and swiftly pulling me aside. He questioned me, saying he had been observing my interactions and asked who I had been talking to. Confused, I explained that I had been conversing with the girl to inquire about her well-being and offer assistance. The man's next words sent shivers down my spine. He revealed that the girl I was referring to was not there, suggesting she was the ghost of a girl who had tragically died in a road accident 26 years ago at that very location. He emphasized that it was fortunate I had not given her any of my belongings, as it would have resulted in grave consequences beyond my imagination. He urged me to continue straight home without stopping.

Shaken and overwhelmed, I ran as fast as I could until I reached the safety of my home. Upon my arrival, my mother opened the door and noticed the distressed state I was in. She questioned me about the girl accompanying me, assuming she was a friend. Unable to process her words, I entered the house and locked myself in my room. That night, sleep eluded me as I tried to calm my racing thoughts. Eventually, exhaustion took over, and I fell into a restless slumber.

When morning arrived, I woke up with a realization. I was incredibly fortunate not to have given my handkerchief to the girl. If I had, she might have pursued me, just like the apparition that had accompanied me the previous night. I remain immensely grateful to the old man who intervened and saved me from a potentially disastrous encounter.

Made in United States
Troutdale, OR
12/01/2024